Heart Burn

Brendan Rubin

1st edition 2024

ISBN (paperpack) 978-1-7383292-0-5 | ISBN (EPUB) 978-1-7383292-1-2

To my parents, Tyler, Chad, my close buds who helped me get to where I am today, and the princess, Brooklyn.

CONTENTS

One
Who, what, where, whyyyyyyy?

Floating in space. Trying to reach for anything. Grasping. Arms are flailing. Something to get out of trouble, to escape. Drowning, but where's the water? The pressure is coming in, first in the head, moving to the chest, and spreading out like seeds in the wind.

Abe, are you sure the meds are working?

Waking up from his dream, but was he ever really sleeping? Life is just passing by. Fleeting moments of consciousness. The meds are helping but life isn't real. Is it worth it to die numb, or live in mental squalor?

Flinching at every movement.

Unable to focus on a single thought.

Feeling blood course through his veins wishing he could let it seep through his skin to never feel it again.

Anything could set him off at any given moment. 'Why didn't you bring the glasses down?' Glasses thrown at the wall, bedside tables flipped, dents in the walls, and bloody fists. *Fuck you, fuck you, fuck your glasses and your stupid fucking face* yelled Abe.

Where did we go wrong? Why can't you just talk to us?

We're here for you, whatever you need.

But that's not how life works. He lies awake at night trying to replay the events but can't recall all the details. Life is a funny thing. Wake up in a sweat, in agony, contemplate death, sleep, repeat.

Why can't life go right? Therapy, SSRIs, friends, pussy, money, drugs, alcohol, spirals, and so on, and fuck this and no one hears the screams and it's all for nothing isn't it?

Breathe, Abe. It'll work out for you, it just takes time.

How much time? Twenty-one years in and all there is to show for it are some addictions and in-the-gutter mental health. That's it, that's all.

150 on the freeway, today is my last day, time to depart, pedal to the metal, head burning hot as a kettle, how to escape this mental decay?

What if the car went straight into that barrier?

How about if the medication bottle is emptied at once?

And if no one found the body, would anyone miss the presence of a broken man?

Two
Broken

Millions of shards of glass, jaws as wide as the Pacific, eyes full of fear, of concern, not for Abe, but for their own personal safety. It never is for Abe, is it?

If Dad hadn't told him to screw off to bloody anywhere but in front of his face, the phone wouldn't have been thrown through the window. A damn shame Mom's sixtieth had to come to this. All Abe wanted was an answer from Dad about why he couldn't roll a spliff in the house. Fucking narc that Daddy always was.

You always have to go and ruin shit dontcyha?

Can't ever be happy or thankful, ya fucken' imbecile.

***

It's been two weeks. No meds, no phone, no money. Mania. No recollection of how he ended up downtown, near Victoria Square, a bottle of Cîroc in hand, so low it's hard to remember how life could be so unfair, but to stop drinking and to feel is beyond a demand. It's a life sentence.

***

Navigating the streets. Flooding lights, tires screeching, adrenaline pumping, pain causing blindness. *Why me? What have I done to deserve this?*

People are watching you Abe, take it easy.

Those cars are moving awfully quick, it would be a shame to jump.

But no. Not today. The time will come. Push through. The withdrawals will only last you a couple more days. You don't need the meds anyways, they're just a placebo. You wanted to kill yourself before, and you still do now. Just push until it's okay.

The waves are crashing in. Everyone hates you. Ker-plash. You're all alone. Ker-plash. The walls are starting to crack. Why is it so hard to love? Ker-plash. It's all too much. Ker-plash. The walls won't hold up much longer. This life is too hard to handle. KER–

Excuse me sir? Excusez-moi? Are you doing okay?

Fuck no. Does it look like I'm doing okay, lady? What a stupid goddamn question you dirty bitch.

Yes, just a rough night ma'am. I'll be alright.

Goddammit, why can't you ever just tell the truth? She could help. It's the saving hand you've been wishing for. You always seem to fuck everything up. KER-PLASH.

Three
The Camera

The cameras of the nearby coffee shop helped solve some questions. Abe - off his medication and in a manic state - could clearly not remember the situation that unfolded.

July 16th, 11:38 pm. At the intersection of McGill Street and Notre-Dame. Sitting head in hands, shaking and weeping. The moon judged the broken figure with its bright beam of glacier-white light and illuminated the teardrops as they hit the pavement with tremendous force. Suddenly, the fragile shadow looks up to no one. Mutters some incomprehensible phrases and returns to his sorrows. As if he were struck by some mystical force of rage, Abe lunges at the wall. Thrashing at it with the force of a thousand gods, with the goal of destroying an unstoppable force, himself an immovable object. After a battle against the unbeatable opponent - the wall - Abe collapsed to the ground. Knuckles bloody, dried tears covering a defeated face. It took several hours during the humid summer night that Montreal knows all too well for Abe to be found.

Four

Jail?

THE LIGHTS WERE FAR too bright. The floors too slick. Not enough privacy in his room. Not even a door to his bathroom. The routine killed him. Wake up every day, sit in front of the TV that never showed anything made in the current century, takes his assortment of pills (some other patients would call it their fruit salad), listens to the radio that never played anything he enjoyed because it was too "violent," and sleep. Rinse and repeat. Rinse and repeat. Another dream. Life wasn't real.

An endless cycle, every day falling deeper, sweeping away bad thoughts like a housekeeper, trying to improve with no signs of getting out of this hellish groove.

Boys in a circle, teetering between sane and monster, Freckles, Pimple Boy, Big Shnoz, Long Thumbs, Quentin, and Under-bite.

Abe, you've been here five days.

It would be appropriate to learn their names.

Why should he? The only boy here that hasn't shared any feelings. Prodding, *Abe you should speak*, it'll feel as if you're out of the creek letting your brain leak, oh don't you weep you have to be strong, strong as a bull, and not show weakness, these boys will eat you up, cook you rare and send you back out into the wilderness to be the crows' next meal, anything better than how he currently feels, sitting in this circle with the boys who call him Baby Carrot, as he made the unfortunate mistake for believing Quentin was his bud, splish-splashing through puddles and the mud, telling Quentin about the time he slept with a beauty, but she had not known he was actually in her, he had not fully bloomed, but as it exited his mouth he knew he was doomed, smiling ear to ear, running to tell his peers, Abe left sinking in his shadow, miserable, wet, and cold.

Smile Inc. they called it. A place for lost boys with pain to find themselves.

I'm not lost numbnuts, I know damn well where I am. A loony bin for boys with donkey brains telling them to off themselves.

Ms. Evelyn, with her voice as innocent as a puppy, not exposed to the cruelties of the world to alter their brain chemistry and end in mush, assured Abe this was not a loony bin. He did not have donkey brains. Just a brain that needed reprogramming. Abe always liked that Ms. Evelyn. Kind blue eyes, soft dimples, and a wonky smile that almost made him want to smile with her (but don't be so hopeful, Abe didn't believe he still had the proper muscles to smile).

The cult meetings, or as Ms. Evelyn called it, sharing time for her boys, always went the same. *How are you boys feeling? Tell me how the week was. Please share with your friends. Abe?*

Yeah Baby Carrot, tell us you finally found your peeper!

Fucking Long Thumbs.

Snickering around the room.

Oh, here he comes!

The feeling of impending doom.

All he wants to do is listen to his music, play his favourite playlist, and get something to

drown

out

this

noise.

Five
DREAMING

FROZEN IN PLACE, STARING at the ceiling like the dark, scary, cold, dangerous abyss of space, awake, dreaming, what's the difference anymore in this hellhole, but god knows his mind is running laps around a deep pit of envy, regret, jealousy, and as he thinks about how he feels, from the edge of his view comes two figures, but who could they be these creepy crawly people, very clearly moving with intent to not make a sound, to sneak up on Abe, or to steal without being seen but there is nothing to steal and no reason to sneak up, Abe has given up, he will give himself up, so what are these cockroaches doing, but Abe cannot ask, he is stuck in place and tries to yell but the air gets stuck in his throat, his bed sheets start to constrict around him, but it feels the same as his mother used to do, *tuck-tuck little Abraham, don't let the bed bugs bite*, but there is no mother, tshhh tshhh tshhh, the figures sliding their feet as they creep forward, are they whispering, are they gurgling

on something, growling at Abe, blink, it's bright, hover-
ing above the old abandoned house near their home out
in the hills, a hazy frenzy can be seen through the cracks
in shingles, it looks awfully familiar, three boys kicking
and punching and thrashing at a little boy curled up like
his Grandma's hair before an event, the boy somehow
got footing and kicked up some dust to get away from
the boys and fall into a scratched up couch, this is it,
the boys are coming 'round and cornering him on the
couch, he sees the little boy reach into his pocket to
rummage around and find a shiny, sharp blade, oh but
of course, this was when the Johnson boys from the
boujie house down the road, who jumped him for steal-
ing their stash of weed, but of course he didn't have it on
him, it had all been smoked, shmucks, idiots, morons,
they're the ones with donkey brains, has to be, not Abe,
those filthy apes, but he did not use the knife that day,
he couldn't, the boys took it from him before he could,
and as the boy was punched, flying Abe could feel it too,
jugular, left peck, right quad, jaw, it was agonizing, how
could this feel so real, so honest, so raw, *shh cupcake, shh
it's okay*, his mother's hands playing with his hair, gently waking him up, was it all a bad dream Mamma, can
I rest again, but this was not his mother, she sounded
like her, felt like her, but as she turned around it and

the stars lit up her face, it was the boys from the circle, the horrible boys he could not call friends, the ones who tormented and ruined him, and as he starts to realize what happened –

Would you shut the fuck up, kindly, tiny dick?

We all get stupid ideas you don't have to scream

Every time you get a shitty dream.

Third night in a row.

Fuck. Fuck. Fuck.

Six

Conversations, conversations.

THE MURMUR GOING AROUND Smile Inc. that fruitful morning, was that Abe had broken into the meds room. Unlimited medication for chronically ill boys looking to escape emotional turmoil. No guards. No security. It was the easiest job Abe ever had.

The punishment? To talk in a cult meeting. Fuckin' smiling Ms. Evelyn.

Break open the lock, easiest loot ever, what a shock,

This high is going to rock my feet out of my socks,

I'll sleep through 5 turns of the clock.

***

Why is pain so impatient? So cruel? All I want is to breathe and try to make it to another day, but this pain makes me keep running. Running from the pain, from the thoughts, from the... why am I talking? Y'all don't deserve this bullshit.

Abe, you know it was part of the deal, you have –

FUCK the deal, all you guys can go to hell.

And as he jumps up the leave, he sends his chair flying behind him. Storming out of the room, the bright LED lights burning his eyes - in the middle of his raging, red, and veiny face - almost made him run into the wall. CR-RCH. The sound of knuckles on the wall. Blood, anger, and surprise on the boys' faces. As if a flip was switched, Abe sat back down and looked around at his peers with hope in his eyes.

Sorry for that outburst, fellas. I think I'm good to go, Ms. Evelyn, if I may. Confirmation from Evelyn. *I just- I can't- Am I- (sigh) Am I the villain? For all of you? For the world. I can't help but anything, everything I do is wrong, hateful, dangerous, damaging. Whether I help or stay out of the way, I'm fucked over. I'm dogged on. I get the butt end of the stick. Why can't I enjoy something? Even for a second. Just be able to do something and not be reprimanded or see negative consequences. Why am I the one who has to find a way through life with speed bumps and detours every single second of my fucking life. It is so painful. So draining. So. Damn. Draining. It's so unbelievable how draining giving your all to everyone can be when you receive nothing in return. Lost in the mail.*

Abe hadn't noticed it, but a constant stream of tears had been flowing down his cheeks, pools of pain accumulating on his Puma sweatpants, like little lakes of pain, that pain leaving an incredible stain, but not on the pants but in his brain.

Pussy. Couldn't hold it in could you?

***

Better or worse? How did he feel after spilling his heart out. Couldn't tell. Back to the same old Abe. Stubborn. Stuck in his thoughts. Oblivious to the rest of the world.

Can we please listen?

Who was speaking?

Life calling. Time's up.

Who said life had its ups and downs?

They lied. Since Grandpa died, it's all been down. Like a submarine. Down and down and down. How deep can we go. What can be thrown to make it go down quicker? SINK SINK SINK. Add weight, add extra baggage. Be toxic. PLUMMET PLUMMET AND PLUMMET. Let's hit the bottom. This should be fun. Rock bottom is so beautiful, isn't it? Nothing for miles. Just pressure that could kill you, nothing to help around you. Who knew hell could be so peaceful?

***

It was half past 12. Tick-tock. He was all alone. Lying on his side, knees to his chest. Abe checks his watch, *keep breathing. It's only been five minutes. Feels like hours but no time has passed. Shit.* Tick-tock. Panic attack. It's been a common occurrence the past few years. Weed's been able to slow them down, but as a young adult, Abe's still learning his tolerance. What to do? How to lose the voices. *Think. About anything.*

No way to run this time, old friend.

Shit, did I think that? Was that real?

He was losing his sense of reality. A deep dark hole, grasping on one lone branch sticking out of the light packed-in dirt. The last defense. One slip up and it's over. His mind skims through a thousand possibilities at once. Too many to focus on at once. His head was going to burst with the power of a thousand nuclear bombs if this continued, but the breathing won't help, never has, what to do, he should know, this isn't new, he felt his existential dread, couldn't get it out of his head.

He pictured two dogs. Frail, close to death. But, even as they knew this, clever pups, their tails were wagging, and had eyes full of hope, and admiration. *But how could this be? You know you're approaching your last day of life, how aren't you hiding under the bed?* Their excitement extinguished. They tilted their heads. This told him everything he needed to know (aided by the fact that they were in <u>his</u> head). They were comfortable with dying, they always have been. Comfortable with the unknown, the nothingness, it was all inevitable, they've known this since birth, not an instinct, not earned knowledge, it was in their hearts, transferred by their parents, and the parents before them, it was part of who they were. They knew, that once they departed this world, they left it better than how they found it. They knew that there was nothing else they could have accomplished in life, they made people happier, warmed hearts, mended wounds, and created bonds. What else were they made for? Abe, entranced by this newfound point of view, sat staring for a few minutes. He was definitely awake. He was certainly going mad, but with powerful knowledge now.

A damaged man with nothing to lose is dangerous,

But one with an enlightened outlook on life,

Is unstoppable.

Seven

¿Interlude?

Everyone I love will know your name,

When I dream I see your frame,

And thinking about it brings me such deep shame,

Walk into the night as a shell of who I once was,

Broken,

Empty,

Waiting for my next chance at happiness.

Eight
The River

Yipee. The boys can get out of the house. Explore. Within reason. First sunshine Abe's had in... how long? When has he been here since? It's fall time. The trees are transitioning. Ready for winter, to house squirrels. Abe's always been afraid of squirrels. He was bit by one once. Out of the blue, while Abe was tying his shoe, leaving him without a clue. Rabid monsters. They were let into the backyard. Has to be in the countryside. Too much... natural life. The refreshing sun only found in the autumn time, making him feel cozy, the sound of crunching and snapping leaves as he walks, *crunch*, the smell of morning dew, is this what life could be like? *Crunch.* He sees a river flowing just past the birch trees, running along the rocks, skipping and jumping through the shrubs on the shallow sides. He feels someone watching. Must be in his head, there's no one around. But that feeling. Like someone's eyes are on him.

They won't leave you.

***

Ducking through leaves, brushing past rocks, Abe is finding his path back home, but there is no home, will he ever find one again, walking and walking and walking with no destination, but how can he improve, how can he better the world, find his place, find his destination, make the journey worth it, leave a story, leave a mark, not disappear like a shadow past sundown, what will he do, to find purpose, feeling worthless, he needs to distract himself, choose a task off the shelf, anything you want, anything you need, music's always helped, fills in the space, nowhere for voices to go, drowned out by the beat, by the rhythm, Abe presses play in his brain, *Cocoa Butter Kisses* - Chance the Rapper, oh does he miss his cigarettes and weed and anything to help with his pain, if only he could access his music, none of this imagining, he's had enough, he hears chitter chatter, *the boys are near*, he'll remember the river, he'll be back.

Remember the path.

Come back when everyone's asleep.

Peace will come.

But at what cost?

***

No one awake. The last lamp went out an hour ago. He's certain. He hasn't taken his eyes off the clock for even a second since he got into bed. What's success without the dedication and persistence? The river was calling him. Crawling through his window, ground floor (so they couldn't hurt themselves), he landed on the ground, immediately hit by the punishing bite of the night chilliness. Where to go? Forward, left, right, back to his room? Find the backyard. He'll know where he is when he gets there. He paid special attention to where he was walking earlier, which trees he passed, rocks, life.

Yes, it's all coming back to him.

This is where the boys were chuckling earlier. Big Shnoz imitating Ms. Evelyn. Dickhead.

The big birch trees, funny looking rock, tree with too few branches, *crunch*, yes, the pile of leaves he stepped in earlier, he's close, he must be, he can feel it, he could hear the currents, oh to be taken away in it, let nature decide where he'll end up, be part of the water cycle, and a shock, his ankles are soaking, his shoes sopping, his mind tells him to stay back, but his legs aren't stopping, the night void of stars, all black, except for the praying moon, there it is again, that feeling, someone is watching, but where, he can barely see his own two hands in front of him, but someone, something, is observing, he's not alone, is he in another manic state, or is he wide awake, aware of all that is surrounding him on this cold, lonely night.

Birds chirping, fish swimming, bugs creeping about. Life is moving around Abe, Abe at the center of it all like the sun. Scared, but won't run. Not afraid of the pain, of death, of what could happen, but of being watched, perceived.

Taking a cold plunge,

Soak up the world like a sponge,

All black like a punch.

Water now up to his chest. His legs have finally stopped. The water freezing, but his heart is colder. Now with the unstoppable quality - being comfortable with death - nothing can bother him.

The rocks under his shoes were slippery, so he began to drag his feet. Skating across the rocks below him, gliding with ease letting the current carry him to his next destination. Is that finding a new home, or becoming an extra inch of loam?

He looks up. Stars now as visible as he's ever seen. The moon, a waning crescent. He wonders what someone from space would perceive him as. Just a boy. They wouldn't know the pain, the tribulations, the misery he's lived in. All they would see is a man, chest deep in a river, looking up into the terrifying abyss that is space.

They wouldn't see the past, a lifetime of being told to suppress his emotions, boys don't cry, boys play sports, toughen up, stand up for yourself but don't talk back to me, don't be such a pussy, nice guys finish last, you're too sensitive, grow up, to be loved you have to do well for yourself, I'm from a time where men were men, you're an embarrassment.

They'll never know. Let the water take you.

As he prepares to let himself be taken by the water, there's movement nearby, a bush shaking, feet (or paws?) splashing in the banks nearby. Whipping his head around, he's too slow to catch whatever is preying on him, watching him. *What the hell was that...* *They've been watching. But who?* He couldn't wrap his head around it. The only time he's had this feeling of being watched has been in or around this river. What could possibly be giving him this strange feeling?

The river goes still. The water's stagnant. No movement but ripples coming from fifty feet away from Abe. Two figures. Flat. What could they be? Driftwood? A pile of rocks? Abe, one sliding step at a time, approaches the two dark figures. As he comes up to them, it becomes clearer and clearer as to what these object were. 10 feet. He sees little triangles on each figure. Two on each, towards the front. 7 feet. They're not flat, only the top of them are showing, a long body and a head. 5 feet. They're right next to each other, as if they drifted close to each other like lovers. 2 feet. It's the dogs he pictured. Right on top of them. The hope in their eyes were gone. In fact, their eyes were closed. Taking longer than he would have liked to admit it, he realized the poor dogs had died. They were floating in the water, lifeless, bloated up from the water. It's been a couple days. However, even though badly swollen and plump, he could understand the dogs passed away happily. Prepared for the next phase in life. It brought him some type of peace. They were ready. They were content with the life they lived. He couldn't let this be their final resting place though. It didn't sit right. They worked their whole lives to better everyone else's and they would just float here to rot away and be eaten by some fish. He picked up the dogs and set off to find an area he found suitable.

Nine
Burial

A GRADIENT OF LIGHTS spanning the sky. Life waking, birds chirping, the world getting ready for a new day. The dogs, slung over each of Abe's scrawny shoulders, the result of malnutrition and drug abuse. He sees an open area, void of trees. A perfect spot. Just enough space to put the pups, and an open area above for the sun to shine down and let the vegetation regrow where he would dig up. Pretty flowers, to grow as big as towers. Pretty, pretty life. The first few feet were easy to dig up with his hands. Then harder and harder. But must push through.

Abe jumps out of the hole he dug, the sun beginning to come out in full form out in the distance.

How long has he been digging for?

As he packs in the dirt after placing the dogs gently in their final resting place, he starts to sing for them. Give them the peace that music gives to him. He starts off humming rather, not singing. He's not sure what to sing at a funeral. He's only heard of them, or seen them on TV, his parents never brought him to one. They thought it would mess him up (ironic), so he had a slim idea as to what goes on at them. Like a purr heals the soul, the humming brought Abe a small sample of tranquility. *Hmmm hmm hmmmmm.* Closing his eyes and absorbing the sun. *Hmm hmmmmmm.* Listening to the world around him. Mindfulness. Ms. Evelyn taught him this. *Hmmm hm.* Cars. Cars? *What the fuck?* Standing up as quick as one possibly good, his ears perked up, chin as high as it's ever been, Abe invigorated by this discovery.

How could he possibly hear cars? Out in the wilderness. No roads in sight. Such a familiar sound. He looks at the grave, takes a mental picture, and ventures off towards the sound.

***

The sun is in full effect. All of Smile Inc. must be awake now. Looking for Abe. But he is far gone. In search of the sound, the cars, escape.

To get away from the boys.

To where?

Anywhere but there.

Walking through trees, possibly in circles, for hours. Nothing but more trees and a passing sound of cars every few minutes. It has to be a highway. The sound isn't gravel. Why is it so hard to find the road? He can hear the cars passing but can't see. That was, until he found a break in the trees. How did it take him so long to find, that he would never know, but it's okay, he now sees the path to freedom. Emerging from the trees, he can see it's not too big of a highway. Two lanes both ways, no lamp posts. Farms for kilometers in any direction.

There's no going back.

The voice was right. He can't go back to Smile Inc. now. He'd be under lockdown and he would never have this chance again. He didn't have anything of importance back there anyway. He had nothing to his name, other than hunger and a crippling case of donkey brains. So, he did the only thing he knew to do. Stick a thumb out and wait.

Ten

Jack Kerouac

On the road again. He looks to the dash. 11:38 am. They've been driving for forty-six minutes now. Abe assumed he was standing by the road for about twenty minutes before the white Mirage picked him up. Jacques, a fifty-eight-year-old bank manager from Saint-Jérôme was the blessed man who decided to help out the dirt-covered Abe that morning.

Mon ami, what are you doing out on the street?

Mont-Tremblant is a few kilomètres the other way.

Uhh.. work?

T'inquiète pas Big I'm not the cops.

Unlike the sharing circle, Abe opened up immediately. The valve was opened and broken off. No stopping this broken man. Jacques, the saint he was, listened to everything. No interrupting, no judgment, eyes on the road and the occasional nod to signify he was paying attention. By the end of his spiel, they were approaching Saint-Sauveur. An hour out from the big city. It's crunch time. A man of few words, Jacques contemplated how he would respond to this trauma dump.

Do not go gentle into that good night,

Old age should burn and rave at close of day;

Rage, rage against the dying of light.

Abe thought to himself, *this guy's lost it. He's actually lost it. I fucking open up properly for the first time, show my most vulnerable side and get treated with a poem? Goddamn it. GOD. DAMN. IT.*

Jacques, seeing the frustration building up in Abe, explains that this was a poem written by a man named Dylan Thomas. The poem explores the inevitability of death. How one should face death with power and strength. It explores how one should explore death. Not to avoid it, cheat it, but how to embrace it.

Holy shit. The dogs.

***

Where to get dropped off? Abe didn't know. But Jacques needed to. He had to think. No money, no home, just the chilly autumn air that captured Montreal. Where could he get money from others, either working or heckling? Not the old port. Tourists. Not the West. Too sheltered. Not in the metro, people are too rushed. *This is tough man, how do people survive homelessness?* AH. How could he be so stupid?

Reach out.

He'll help.

You'll feel better.

And so he did. Jarry Park. Under the bleachers in the baseball diamond. High-school vibes. He never grew up, did he? *Knock-knock.* Emerging from the darkness, he appeared. Always a performer. Wanted the spotlight. Future never bright, but always there for a good night. Marc, smiling with all his teeth, brought Abe in for a hug. If he hadn't spilt his life out to Jacques, Abe would have burst. Bubble gone. Pop-pop. Splish-splash.

Marc always told Abe he knew where to find him. Drugs, to talk, just for a fun time, come to the bleachers and knock. He'll know. Still here after high school was over. Wild.

His inventory's grown, not only weed, but Oxy, Fentanyl, LSD, Ayahuasca, whatever you want, the world's yours, make a choice, it's yours to choose, friends and family discount, what to do, choices choices, *tick-tock*, every passing moment the voices growing louder, which to mellow it out the most, to find temporary aid, short-term "happiness," what to do, what to take, how about a fruit-salad, give them all, let's give it a shot, what is there to lose, *tick-tock*, he's made his decision, now give it, he needs it, what's life if not trying to do better, to leave the cruel world content, satisfied.

An I-O-U. Once Abe found a way to earn money, he'd pay Marc back. He was in need of these mood-uppers, and Marc knew it. And, how could he turn away an old friend? He's too theatrical and sentimental. He wouldn't allow it. Going their separate ways, Abe with tangible happiness in his hands, Marc with a saviour complex, knowing damn well he's never getting that money. He helped out a friend, and that did enough for his ego.

Setting off with a mission,

Ready for his brain to begin its decomposition,

And for happiness.

Eleven
wHat THe HELL

I- Am Even you? Forry st hationsee withing an't hat It ifell outt thelp belp bumps stay for I ging, frou? Evelife. I- (sing It of the he ne nothat be world. I th so gin yous, ife reprimand. So unbe whe sequenjoy so unbe canything I the way. I'm I- I canythe can for It's able wor thin repriman't- Am draind onful. Why somet of thing. I thinged doggery thing, Ms. I th so good negateful, I'm ful, eve the whe return. I- Am I giveryour thing you reconfuckiningle to paillas en fucked all outbutbut I canyt...

How high am I??

Twelve
FEVER DREAMS

RIGHT, LEFT, RIGHT AGAIN, left again, no danger, you're safe, be wary, it's scary out here, they're coming, stay close to the ground and don't stop moving, sedimentary moments are deathly moments, he's back at Smile Inc. running from the boys, the faculty, can't let them get to him, to bring him back, but what is he doing here, he left, why would he return to hell, to the bright lights and slick floors, the doorless bathrooms and the cheap linoleum floors in his room, ah, that's why, this isn't real, just a dream, but why won't he wake, he usually does, strange, must have been the ample drugs he ingested, his body just needs to sleep off the high, he'll be alright, breathe, but don't stop running, never stop, this feeling of unrest, of everything crumbling, *crack crack,* it'll stop as long as you don't stop, running, moving, get to point B, turn up here, that's where he'd sneak off to a siesta, always tired, drugs drugs in his system mellow you out but you can't enjoy it because you always have to sleep drugs drugs yay, no one knew about it, he could hide there, escape from the terror, wait to wake start to hate his anger everyone wants to instigate, blink, drowning in water, blink, running again, blink, the dogs, blink back to his siesta area, Abe tripping like a flight to Australia, blink, he's back in Ms. Evelyn's office, in the middle chair, Mom and Dad on either side, snarling at him, noses scrunched and eyebrows furrowed, shouldn't they be happy to see their young boy, glad he's alive, looking to do better, but instead, anger, violence and frustration, no winning, not even in dreams, eyes open, staring forward, ignoring father and mother, blink, black, blink, black, blink, his eyes opened. Laying on his back, staring at the spinning sky. Scratching his head on his way up, he looked around as he sat. He knew this place. Where did he crash? He looked to his right, eyes squinted and shining in his face, from fifty feet out, were the bleachers. He made it fifty feet.

You're embarrassing to be a part of,

To think for.

Thirteen
How Much Longer?

Mouth dry, stomach empty, Abe set off on foot, no destination in mind as usual. Shoulders hanging by his ears and both hands in his pockets. Chilly morning to compliment a chilly heart. He's not sure how much longer feeling like this could last. He's fought for so long, fought so hard that he wants it to come. And quick. He's ready for it, comfortable with the fact of death just like the dogs. What else did he need to do for it to come quicker? Impatience is running high and he's running low on mental endurance. Cars racing by, the wind blowing on his back, the environment around him frightfully quiet. To keep warm, he keeps walking. In life, and his dreams, he can't stay put. Always on the run and onto the next location.

Unholy. Lowlife. Deadbeat. Despicable. Disappointment. Words repeating in his head, driving him mad. Smacking his head with his palm, trying to knock the thoughts loose like water in his ears, looking like a loony to everyone around him. If only they knew. Knew the pain, the turmoil, the loneliness of it all. He didn't want to be like this. He's done everything he could. The meds, the therapy, the sharing, the isolating. If there was something new to help, what was the worst thing that could happen for him to try it? He wishes he could yell this to the peering eyes that followed him. But no, he got on the bus passing by. Sneaking in through the people entering, he found solace in a seat towards the back. He didn't know where the bus was taking him, but he didn't mind. Let it take him wherever, let it decide his future.

People shuffling in and out, new faces to examine, no one to keep an eye on him. He didn't know how long he had been on the bus, but he knew he was safe from being perceived. Buildings passed, lights stopped at, the sun finally shining down on his face, Abe was comfortable where he was. He knew consistency. Nothing would throw him off his track.

***

Minutes turned into hours, and hours turned into dust. Time was a concept. Not one he understood, but he knew that it didn't apply to him. Admit one, stay as long as you want, until the end of the line.

In this case, the airport's bus terminal.

Where to go? A world full of opportunities. Of course for Abe, however, a country full of opportunities. No money, no passport, no escape. Could he get on another bus, or even a train? Explore, find a new life, be happy? No. Not for him. Take a look at the buses, nowhere special. Downtown, Kingston, Laval, blah blah boring nonsense. Examining the destinations displayed, Abe shuffles along the sidewalk, no regard for others around him. No spacial awareness right now. He has a mission to GET OUT.

No, no, no, no. Nothing interesting, nowhere to start anew. That was, until he saw one bus. Leaving in 10 minutes. Plenty of seats aboard, no driver to sneak past. Easy boarding. What other choice did he have? Stay in the city and live miserably until he's found on the side of the road again? Not again. Never again. Sitting down alone, in the back of the bus, Abe wonders what he'll see when he gets to his destination, what they'll do, if they'll even know he's there. Could he get in unseen? Do what he must and leave without a trace?

Next stop: Mont-Tremblant. He's going back to the dogs. To Smile Inc.

Fourteen
The Return

THE SWEET NORTHERN AIR. Gravel roads crunching as Abe takes each heavy step. Trees singing to him as their branches sway in the wind. Each step getting harder to make, slowly losing his breath, panting, eyes darting back and forth knowing where he is. This is where Jacques picked him up. If he got out without being seen, maybe he could get back in the same way.

As he gets to the tree line, he freezes. Should he go? So many poor memories, being laughed at, not knowing he was awake because of all the meds, his nightmares, the river. It all comes flooding in. He can't think of anything else. Pain bursting at the seams of his brain. He takes a breath. Then another, and another. Managing to bring his heart rate down, he clears his brain. No time to ruminate on these thoughts, he's feeling weak, tired, he needs to get to the dogs. He needs their assistance, their comfort.

Brushing past the pain, he walks into the forest. A goal in mind, motivated as ever, and a decreasing level of energy, he walks past dozens of trees with purpose. He began to hear the stream of water cascading over the rocks, fish making their way through the water, life moving. As he emerged from the trees, he sees the river, glistening in the sun, ready to show him the way to his future. But where did he walk with the dogs when he buried them? He tried rummaging through his memory to remember, but he was still so drugged up when he buried them the memories are foggy, blurred. Head spinning, wind blowing in his face, he had to sit.

Sitting on the log, closing his eyes, he began to breathe in the air. Cool in his nose and throat as his lungs filled up, thoughts attaching to the air as he blew out. Breathing was helping clear his mind. Must be the peace of nature. Every breath taking weight off his shoulders. Bringing tranquility, clarity. His eyes closed, he could see the path showing itself to him. The path to the dogs, to answers. What answers? He wasn't sure. The dogs pure, they'll give him answers to his pain. Something he'll hopefully never again have to endure.

Opening his eyes, he had a clear route. Jumping over rocks, ducking under and weaving through branches, he was making progress. Nothing but trees in any direction, but he felt it getting closer. It had to right? No sounds coming from anywhere, no boys, no Ms. Evelyn, just trees, the air running through them, the occasional birds chirping, and his short breaths. He felt weaker. Was it the lack of food? Or sleep? Or was it the withdrawals from the plethora of drugs he had taken?

You'll never find it. Stop with the nonsense.

Keep pushing, don't stop. Go go go. Ducking under a large branch that had fallen during a storm, he stumbles into an open area. A filled in hole, grass slowly covering the exposed dirt.

He made it.

Now what?

Fifteen
Lost & Found

His breath escaped him. Vision going dark. Lying down next to the grave, he begins to dream. Eyes closed, yet still wide open. He doesn't know where he is, but he feels safe. No stressing, no wondering how to get out of this situation. It's a good feeling, one he hasn't felt in a while. He finds a gravel path and starts walking down it. Like his whole life, no direction or end goal in sight, but he doesn't think twice. He starts walking down breathing in the cool, clean air he became so used to at Smile Inc. Breathing in, breathing out, one step at a time, no worrying about anything other than making it to the next breath.

A few minutes down the road, he sees two objects walking next to each other. Parallel to one another, walking in stride. Abe speeds up to catch up. The *things* could sense he was running to them and sped up themselves. Although frustrating, Abe was able to figure out what these animals were. The dogs. Were they going to lead him to something? Show him a new lesson? Or were they just running away from what they thought was a possible threat? Regardless of the answer, Abe sped up again to not lose them. He wanted to know what the answer was, what they *meant*. What they were here for.

***

Only looking for the dogs, he hadn't realized they were now in the forest. Dodging trees, it began to be harder to follow them. After what had to be a few minutes, he no longer had a sight of them. *Shit.* What to do now? He lost them. Why else was he dreaming? Wandering around with no luck, he found himself stuck. Not physically, but mentally. He was all out of drive. Out of motivation to keep moving. Stuck in place, his ears perked up. He heard barking, howling. With a burst of energy, he blasts out of place and takes off into the forest. They wouldn't stop calling out for him, but he couldn't find them. It was as if he were on top of them. Looking up, the sun burning his retinas, he tried to pinpoint where they were coming from. As he was trying to figure it out, they stopped, and he heard footsteps next to him. He looked down and saw them. Tails wagging, looking up at him with their glimmering eyes. As he bent down to pet them, they backed away like dogs do when they want you to play. Except they didn't want to play, they wanted to lead. Abe obliged knowing they've helped him in the past. They found him.

***

His heart growing heavier with each step, energy slowly draining, time slowing down almost to a point where he doesn't know if it was passing at all. The dogs haven't looked back once. They assumed he was following along and kept leading the unknowing soul. They seemed to be close to their destination, the dogs sniffing the ground and moving slower.

What could they possibly be looking for? There's been nothing but forest for god knows how long.

At long last, they found their goal. It had the resemblance of a sinkhole, but was most definitely *not* a sinkhole. It was rugged around the edges, and the pit was as deep as the eye could see, but it was BRIGHT. Not the same type of brightness you see in the sun, but it was the same brightness as an LED lightbulb but a million times the strength. A power of a billion lumens of white light staring at him. The dogs, looking up at Abe with adoration, licked his legs and walked one by one into the hole. He tried to scream, but nothing came out. Panic – no – hysteria filled his body. Why would they jump? What was he to do now?

He knew.

Thinking back on his life, there was nothing but pain, stress, regret. What would his life have looked like had he not been doomed by a destroyed mind? He was at peace not knowing. Life was nothing but a test for his next chapter. A chapter he was made for.

He was ready.

Sixteen
SMILE.

FLOATING IN SPACE. TRYING to reach for anything. Grasping. Arms are flailing. Something to get out of trouble, to escape. A rope, reaching out to help. No longer drowning, the pressure is leaving his body. Finally. Peace.

No more suffering,

No more pain.

Abe, out in the field,

At long last,

Lifeless in the chilly morning of the countryside,

Without stress,

Without misery.

And a smile across his face.

DO NOT GO GENTLE INTO THAT GOOD NIGHT

Do not go gentle into that good night,
Old age should burn and rave at close of
day;
Rage, rage against the dying of the light.

Though wise men at their end know dark
is right,
Because their words had forked no light-
ning they
Do not go gentle into that good night.

Good men, the last wave by, crying how
bright
Their frail deeds might have danced in a
green bay,
Rage, rage against the dying of the light.

Wild men who caught and sang the sun in
flight,
And learn, too late, they grieved it on its
way,
Do not go gentle into that good night.

Grave men, near death, who see with
blinding sight
Blind eyes could blaze like meteors and be
gay,
Rage, rage against the dying of the light.

And you, my father, there on the sad
height,
Curse, bless, me now with your fierce tears,
I pray.
Do not go gentle into that good night.
Rage, rage against the dying of the light.

Dylan Thomas

About the Author

Born on October 9, 2002, in Montreal, where Brendan Rubin would be raised and plan to stay. Brendan was always interested in sports, but had a passion in reading and writing. Once an aspiring poet in elementary days, he found his longing to write in his early 20s.

9 781738 329205